BUY BOOK,
GET GUY

BUY BOOK, GET GUY

GET GUY

A Sometimes Politically Incorrect, but Always Truthful, Guide to Men, Women, and Dating

Paul Millman and "The Guys"

A Perigee Book

A Perigee Book
Published by The Berkley Publishing Group
200 Madison Avenue
New York, NY 10016

Copyright © 1997 by Paul Millman
Book design by Rhea Braunstein
Cover design by Joe Lanni
Cover photograph by George Kerrigan

First edition: February 1997

Published simultaneously in Canada.

The Putnam Berkley World Wide Web site address is
http://www.berkley.com/berkley

Library of Congress Cataloging-in-Publication Data
Millman, Paul.
    Buy book, get guy : a sometimes politically
incorrect, but always truthful, guide to men, women,
and dating / Paul Millman and the guys. —1st ed.
        p.   cm.
    "A Perigee book."
    ISBN 0-399-52266-2
    1. Dating (Social customs) 2. Mate selection.
    I. Title.
  HQ801.M57   1997
  646.7'7—DC20   96-21259
                                              CIP

Printed in the United States of America

10   9   8   7   6   5   4   3

Contents

Introduction

"You Should Write a Book . . ."

Unlike virtually every other book about dating, this book is written by *men*, for women.

The authors are not psychologists, social workers, or professional matchmakers. There are no profound psychological lessons intended—it is practical advice based on our years of dating experience and the experiences of our friends and colleagues.

In our discussions with platonic female friends and former girlfriends, the authors have frequently been asked to offer suggestions to help them in their dating lives. We've consistently heard, "You're kidding, I never knew that. . . . You should write a book on dating."

When we'd heard it often enough, we decided to

do exactly that. We believe that single women don't need more dating advice from relationship counselors or therapists. Women need to hear some simple, straightforward advice from the *men* they would like to date. Few books, if any, are written by average, everyday men, with real-life dating experience.

Here's an analogy:

Northern State College has a great football team, largely the result of years of great coaching and re-cruiting. The team's players love the coach, and many have chosen to play for the school because of the coach's unsurpassed reputation. The Northern State team wouldn't trade its coach for any other coach in the world. But next week, the team will be facing Southern State University. Suppose it were possible for the Northern State team to spend a day with the head coach of Southern State. Southern's coach would divulge the contents of Southern's playbook, and reveal their strategies, strengths, and weaknesses. Even the beloved coach of Northern State agrees this would be a day well spent.

Buy Book, Get Guy divulges the opposing team's playbook. After all, who knows what men are think-ing better than men? But there is one significant dif-ference. In football there is always a winning team and a losing team. In the world of dating, everyone is striving for a win–win situation. The Southern State coach would be considered a traitor if he *actually* re-vealed plays to the Northern State team. But when it comes to dating, the male team actually *wants* the female team to have its playbook.

If you are getting all the dates you want, with exactly the men you want, and they're all calling you back, then you don't need this book. However, if that's not the case, you do have choices. You can either continue using the methods you have been employing so far, or decide to make a change. If you have the courage to change, then we have a game plan to help.

Why This Book?

In our conversations with our male colleagues in preparation for writing *Buy Book, Get Guy*, we were struck by one fact. All men, regardless of age, race, occupation, or political affiliation, had sentiments that coalesced around recurring themes.

Women spend fortunes in an effort to meet Mr. Right. They spend money on clothes, makeup, admission to cultural events, and vacations. When they finally encounter an eligible man, they can blow their whole financial and psychic investment of energy by saying or doing just one wrong thing. Unfortunately, one wrong move is sometimes all it takes.

Men encounter the same mistakes over and over, made by otherwise intelligent, charming women. *Buy Book, Get Guy* reveals these mistakes, so that you can eliminate them from your repertoire, and immeasurably improve your "success ratio."

There is one key difference between *Buy Book, Get Guy* and almost all the other books about dating. This book is written from a male perspective, which is to say it is simple and direct. We offer no psycho-babble, no deep strategies for self-analysis, no sugarcoating.

Another illustration:

Sally and Mary are administrative assistants at the same company, making identical salaries. Sally puts no money aside. Mary makes a point of saving fifty dollars per week. After five years Sally has no savings, while Mary has a considerable nest egg.

The point? Over the long haul, *minor* changes in your lifestyle can yield *major* dividends.

Following our advice will not miraculously bring fifty eligible men to your doorstep. However, over time, it *will* increase the odds that you'll meet and marry (if that's your goal) the man of your choice. Integrate just one of the points that follows, and you'll immediately improve your chances with men.

Are You Jennifer?

Jennifer is thirty-three years old and single. She lives and works in Philadelphia, where she is a media buyer for a small advertising agency. Jennifer is intrinsically bright, with a slightly offbeat sense of humor. She has no children, but certainly wants them, as well as a husband and a happy marriage.

Most men consider Jennifer attractive. She has chin-length auburn hair, with a trim figure and "million-dollar" legs. Jennifer has no boyfriend at the moment, but is in the "actively looking" mode. Here are some of her recent experiences.

One of Jennifer's friends introduces her to Tom, an eligible attorney. On their Tuesday-night dinner date, both Tom and Jennifer have an enjoyable time. Tom calls her at her office on Thursday, but Jennifer is busy preparing for a meeting and suggests that Tom call her at home that evening. Tom does call that evening and leaves a message on Jennifer's answering machine. Jennifer gets home at midnight, too late to return the call, and is still too wrapped up in client preparation to return the call on Friday. Tom, assuming that Jennifer is attempting to avoid a weekend date, never calls back.

The following week, Jim, a platonic friend, invites Jennifer to a Friday-night cocktail party in his building. Jennifer spends two hours getting ready. She decides to wear a fashionable pantsuit that unfortunately conceals one of her best physical assets. She spends most of her time at the party with Jim. Every eligible man at the party assumes that Jim and Jennifer are a couple, and steers clear.

Several weeks later, Jason tries to make a date for Thursday night, but Jennifer declines because she's getting together for dinner with her friends Susan and Kathy. The primary topic of dinner conversation revolves around the difficulty of meeting eligible men.

If this is a major topic of conversation for you and your friends, read on.

BUY BOOK, GET GUY

Chapter 1

Ground Rules

This book is *not* about the way things should be. It's about the way they *are*.

Recognize that male behavior is the product of *five million years* of evolution, and you're not going to change it. You can fight it (perhaps a worthwhile pursuit from the perspective of society as a whole) or you can acknowledge it, and thereby improve your own social life. Or you can try to do both, and if you succeed, you can write your own book.

Distinct male-female gender roles are millions of years old. Females could not both nurture their offspring and travel far afield to gather food. This led to male-female pairing—the female caring for the young and the male procuring food. This, in turn, gave rise to the "breadwinner" and "homemaker" differentiation between men and women—a tradition that's only recently been modified.

Responding to the primal drive to perpetuate the species, males sought *fertility*, as signified by specific physical attributes in women. Today, men still look for a woman's physical attributes as a basis for attraction. Females sought *security* in men who had proven themselves to be good providers. In today's words, security often translates into wealth.

You may lament the fact that you have to "play the game" or that men don't seem to appreciate your intellect as readily as they do your body. Nevertheless, that's the way it is, and it's been that way for five million years. Change has been rapid during the past fifty years, but in your dating lifetime, it might be simpler just to go with the flow.

Buy Book, Get Guy's suggestions apply *if* you are trying to enhance your success rate in your relationships with men. Beyond that, the authors would never presume to tell you how to behave or how to live your life.

Be realistic. This book is not about how to get *any* man you want, it's about increasing your chances with men overall.

We assume you can *get* a date. We intend to improve your chances with the men you *want* to date. It's up to you to decide which men you want to attract (you've got hundreds of books and magazine articles to guide you), and after you've attracted them, which men are worthy of your interest and attention.

Understand one eternal truth: Women and men are *different*.

For example, men do not read books like this one. Women are much more likely than men to write, or to read, books about male-female relationships. This is a clue to one of the key differences between the sexes: Women like to *analyze*, men like to *act*.

If you assume *men are pigs*, you'll seldom be disappointed. In recommending the *Sports Illustrated* "Swimsuit" issue to our friends, men do not say, "You'll be impressed by the subtle interplay between the blue of her bathing suit and the highlights of the sunset. . . ."

Don't let men know that's what you're assuming, and don't treat them that way.

Always remember this. You can't teach a pig to sing. You waste your time, and you annoy the pig.

Chapter 2

Your General Attitude

You are a salesperson, and men are your customers.

Imagine you are selling a product and Mr. Smith is your most valued prospect.

- *Would you be late for an appointment with Mr. Smith?*
- *Would you defer a meeting with Mr. Smith because it did not fit conveniently into your schedule?*
- *Would you leave Mr. Smith's voice-mail messages unreturned?*

Enough said.

An important secret in sales is to think from the customer's point of view, and tailor your presentation accordingly.

Another axiom in sales is belief in the product. A positive self-image is essential if you expect men to respond positively to you.

Some women like to construct hurdles for men to clear. In clearing these hurdles, the men validate the woman's sense of self-worth and desirability. Don't construct hurdles. Get your self-validation elsewhere.

Any man that *you* find desirable is probably attractive to other women as well, and has easier alternatives than clearing your hurdles to pursue you.

Another woman, even if she is not equally desirable, will get his attention if she creates fewer roadblocks.

Prophecies, even negative ones, can be self-fulfilling. You may have girlfriends who converse at length about how awful men are, how they'll never meet a good one, and why it's useless even to try. Just as the power of positive thinking enhances our possibilities, the power of negative reinforcement diminishes them. Try to cultivate a group of friends who view men in a more positive light, enjoy their company, and regularly "fraternize with the enemy." You'll definitely have more upbeat conversations, and probably more dates as well.

Don't subscribe to the belief that "all the good men are either gay or married."

Relinquish the idea that your friends take priority over meeting a man. Most of your friends will get married and move on. You will be without friends *or* a man.

We realize that women crave romance. Some women may feel that "playing the percentages" is a very un-romantic notion. To those women, we pose this question: Which is more romantic? To follow an unromantic "strategy" and have a date on Saturday night, or to wait in vain for Prince Charming, alone at home on Saturday night?

You might have heard this advice: "If he doesn't love you as you are, forget him."

Don't forget *him*—forget this *advice*.

Here's an example. Assume you've been offered a

promotion within your company, say, as director of marketing for a new division at a 30 percent salary increase. But there's a catch. One key requirement for this position is proficiency in a computer spreadsheet program, and you've never even had a computer on your desk. Would you decline the promotion or would you enroll in a computer class?

Everyone has areas that can be enhanced, and minor flaws that can be corrected. Doing so will enhance the likelihood of meeting and keeping the right person. On the other hand, if a man thinks your whole persona needs a makeover, clearly it's time to forget him.

Don't let your job, no matter how high-powered, overwhelm your romantic opportunities. If the President of the United States can find time for a romantic dalliance, so can you.

Desperate doesn't sell.

Don't confuse *spontaneous* behavior with *inconsiderate* behavior. Canceling a date at the last minute is not spontaneous, it's rude. Men will interpret an impromptu cancellation as a message to never call again.

Don't let them call you a predator.

Be aware of the difference between *predatory* and *focused*. Men sometimes use the word *predatory* to describe women who are too obviously focused on meeting men. Strive to be perceived by men or women as "gracious" or "outgoing." Be as friendly to women as you are to men.

Now that we've warned you about being predatory, be aware that the very same behavior that men disdain as predatory in females is considered perfectly acceptable when displayed by other men. Remember, 5 million years of evolution.

At the risk of sounding like "Miss Manners," we should point out that graciousness wears incredibly well—little things like saying "please" when asking a waiter for a second glass of water, and "thank you" when your date holds open the door for you. The last time "manners" were taught may have been in elementary school, but believe us, men notice, appreciate, and remember.

In dating, there is no such thing as success by association. Your father may be a prominent attorney, or your aunt a renowned businesswoman. But coming from a "good family" means little if you don't have your own accomplishments to stand on.

Any suitor who is overly concerned with your family background may be motivated by money and not romance. He may be more interested in your "dowry" than in you.

You wouldn't bank on winning the lottery as a way to fund your retirement. Similarly, don't bank on Mr. Right (whom you've never met before) charging out of his limousine, roses in hand, into the restaurant where you and your friends are dining, interrupting your dinner conversation, and pledging his eternal devotion.

Meeting Men: Rules of Engagement

Meeting men is an essential prerequisite to dating them.

Get out of the house. You may think your chances of meeting a man on the elevator or in the super-market are small, but your chances of meeting a man in your living room are *zero*.

Many of our female friends have confided to us that the man they ultimately married did not "fit the mold" that they had always envisioned for themselves. And they were not disappointed. Don't rule out the man across the room because he doesn't conform to your preconceived notion of what your future husband should look like.

Be optimistic. Oddly enough, there is no correlation between a man's attractiveness and his opinion about you. He might be a nerd, yet not think highly of you. On the other hand, you might consider him unapproachable, and he might find you desirable.

Sometimes, it's OK to make the first move.

You may be weary of pickup lines and unsolicited

gestures. However, most *men* are flattered when a woman makes the first move.

Think of the approaches that you find tiresome. Men often find these very same gestures refreshing, charming, and flattering because they encounter them so rarely. So if it suits your temperament, take the extra step. (This is especially important if you perceive that your appearance might be intimidating to the men you want to approach you.) Send over a drink in a restaurant. Smile and say "hi" to the guy walking his dog in front of your building. If you're standing on line next to an appealing man at the Department of Motor Vehicles, try commenting about the improvement in service since the last time you were there.

Our friend Miriam offers this observation: There may be smarter or prettier women in the room, but very few will walk up to a desirable man, smile, and say, "Hi, I'm Miriam Morningstar." Remember: You're doing the man a favor by introducing yourself.

There are many protective devices that women use to shield themselves in public. These include stereo headphones, dark sunglasses—even the company of other men and women. If you are comfortable in public without these devices, you enhance the likelihood that you'll be approached by men who would otherwise be discouraged by these barriers. And remember, men are *everywhere*.

Identify your own, personal level of "outgoing-ness."

Here's an example. You're in a Chinese restaurant. The attractive man at the adjacent table leans over and asks you the name of the dish that you're eating.

Level 1: You respond, "Chicken and Broccoli," and resume eating.

Level 2: You respond, "Chicken and Broccoli. It's very good here, but be sure to tell them no MSG."

Level 3: You respond, "Chicken and Broccoli. It's very good here. Would you like to try some? By the way, my name is Darlene . . ."

Level 4: Rather than waiting for him to initiate the conversation, you begin by asking him, "That dish you're eating looks delicious. Where is it on the menu?"

What's your current comfort level, *1,2,3,* or *4?* If you can crank up your comfort level just one notch, you'll dramatically increase your opportunities.

Here's another example with a different twist.

A male friend of ours has a "patented" method for meeting women at the beach. He approaches a woman on her blanket, and while maintaining a respectful distance, mentions that he is on his way to the food concession (usually a good distance down the beach), and asks if she would like him to bring back anything for her.

On two consecutive weekends several years ago, he received two contrasting responses:

Woman 1: "No, thank you."

Woman 2: "Oh, that's *sooo* nice of you to offer. I don't want anything, but I really appreciate your asking. I'll be here, so feel free to stop by on your way back to your blanket. . . ."

As our friend discovered later, *both* women actually had an interest in him.

Woman 2's interest was clearly expressed in the graciousness of her response, and they went out later that week.

Oddly enough, Woman 1 was also interested in our friend. We know this because they had a chance encounter at a party several years later, dated, and eventually married. In this case, there was a happy ending because of their fortuitous (but unlikely) meeting at the party.

Generally, most of us don't get enough second chances to be cavalier about our first encounters.

You can almost always tell when an overture is coming. If you're interested, be friendly. If you even think you might be interested, be friendly enough to keep your options open until you decide one way or the other.

If you'd prefer not to trust your life to the winds of fate, aim for a higher level of interaction. There was no duplicity required of either Woman 1 or Woman 2. Both women were telling the truth. Neither woman wanted anything from the food concession, but Woman 2 was alert enough to turn an unexpected encounter to her advantage.

If you're initiating a conversation in a public place, such as a restaurant or supermarket, avoid putting the man in a potentially uncomfortable situation. Don't

violate accepted norms of personal space. Don't phys-
ically corner your target between the asparagus and
the frozen food. Especially if you're making the first
move, leave the man some breathing room. Know
when the encounter is over—be sensitive to his body
language and verbal clues.

Don't begin a conversation on a negative note. If
you're at a party and see a man that interests you,
don't say, "You look uncomfortable here," or refer
to the rest of the guests as "a group of misfits" because
they may very well be his close friends. An insensitive
opening line is probably worse than no opening line
at all. There are so many complimentary ways to start
a conversation, why lead with something negative?
Try a positive approach like one of these:

*"My friend and I have a bet about your tie. She says it's
Armani, I think it's Polo. Can you settle it for us?"*
or
*"I'm going over to the dessert table. If you save my seat,
I'll bring some back for you."*

Note-passing can be a useful technique.

You're in a restaurant and you see a man you think you'd like to meet, but he's unapproachable because he's with another woman, or is part of a larger group. If your instincts tell you he's available, but you can't be absolutely sure of the status of his relationship with his companion(s), compose a simple note that identifies you and leaves a phone number for further contact, in case he's interested in following up. Ask your waiter to deliver the note at a discreet moment. You may be pleasantly surprised.

Stick to your strengths. In baseball, if you're a fastball hitter and you swing at curveballs, your batting average will likely plummet. Similarly, if you're forty, and choose to pursue the twenty-five-year-old intern at the hospital where you work, you might be disappointed. Select appropriate targets and you'll achieve a higher success rate.

Judging interest:

- A man *is not* interested if . . .
  he avoids eye contact at all costs.
- A man *is* interested if . . .
  he is making (or trying to make) eye contact.
- A man *may be* interested if . . .
  he does neither of the above.

If you *sense* a man is interested, he probably *is* interested.

When you start your car in cold weather, sometimes the engine doesn't turn over immediately. Then, after a few cranks, it starts. Similarly, the chances of success are not always apparent in the first moments of conversation or the first dates of a relationship. You may have to give it a few tries before you know for sure if it's going to work.

Sometimes, however, your car battery is just dead. Look for *chemistry*, and recognize it when it exists. If the chemistry is there, almost any method of introduction will work. If there's absolutely no chemistry, recognize it and move on.

A popular comedian has a routine in which he recounts his lack of success in meeting the right woman. His relatives are always telling him, "Don't worry. It'll happen when you least expect it . . . when you're not even trying. . . ." To which he responds, "What do you mean? . . . I'm *always* trying."

The comedian is right. As a rule, men are *always* trying to meet women.

In jujitsu, the ancient art of self-defense, you are trained to achieve victory by leveraging your opponent's greater force to your own advantage. Similarly, in almost any chance encounter, a woman can use the momentum of a man's mating instinct to her own advantage. The slightest bit of encouragement on your part will usually sustain the man's pursuit. In most cases, all you need to do is *not walk away* and the man will do most of the work.

In any situation, whether a business negotiation or personal encounter, it's advisable to know in advance what you want the outcome to be.

During any chance encounter with a man, try to decide quickly whether you have any interest. Err on the liberal side, you can always say no later on. If you decide that you are interested, encourage him. Keep the conversation going, and offer subtle indications of your interest—smile, look directly into his eyes, appear intrigued by what he's saying. As noted above, this will probably not be too difficult.

Here's an example. You're in the crowded electronics section of Macy's at Christmastime. You're attempting to discern the difference in TV picture quality between the RCA and the Magnavox, when you feel a slight jolt. You turn quickly to discover the source—a handsome gentleman, with no wedding ring, apologizing for having accidentally bumped into you. You make a split-second assessment of the situation and determine that this is a man in whom you might possibly be interested. You're now in a position to offer a response more engaging than a simple "no problem"—a response that might ultimately lead to a sustained conversation and a date. For example, you might respond: "That's OK . . . and as long as you're here let me enlist your opinion . . . which of these two pictures looks sharper to you?" The man will certainly offer some response, and you can take it from there.

Don't wear stereo headphones at the gym. It sends a signal that you are unapproachable.

At social gatherings, don't cluster in large, impenetrable groups of five or six women. Men would rather walk barefoot across hot coals than brave rejection in front of a half dozen women.

If you are out with a platonic male friend, here are some techniques to make it clear to other men that you are available:

- Make eye contact.
- Lie. Loudly refer to your companion as "Cousin Bob" or ask "Where is Aunt Ida going on vacation? . . ."
- Ask your platonic male friend to introduce you to any interesting prospects.

Make your girlfriends your allies, not your rivals.

Work in tandem with a girlfriend. If you're at a party and there's a man that interests you—let's call him Mr. Target—have your friend walk over and position herself near him. A few moments later, you saunter over, give your friend a big hello, and presto, you're within conversational distance of Mr. Target. Your friend's position gives legitimacy to *your* presence there. At this point, you can hope that Mr. Target begins a conversation with you, or you can initiate one with him.

Network. The more people you know (and who know you), the greater your chances of meeting someone or being introduced to someone.

An inebriated woman is not charming. After you've had a "few too many" is not the best time to introduce yourself to the cute guy playing pool at the far end of the room.

Picture this. You're at a party, and you've just given your telephone number to a man. Five minutes later you see him, just a few feet away, exchanging phone numbers with yet another woman. Think about how you'd feel in this situation. Similarly, don't put yourself in a situation where a man can easily observe you dispensing your phone number to multiple men.

Have a party.

- A party provides a perfect opportunity to widen the net, and it's the perfect excuse to approach men you might not otherwise approach. For example, invite the interesting guy you've seen at the supermarket twenty times before. He'll be flattered, and will probably accept your invitation. Even if he doesn't, you'll have broken the ice, and he may even ask you out directly.
- There's another payback. You'll be invited to parties of the people you invite to your party, where there will be even more men to meet.
- A few things to remember. Be sure to invite a roughly equal number of men and women. If you have too many men (no such thing?) they will quickly observe the imbalance, and will equalize it for you by leaving.
- Organizing a book club or charitable fund-raising drive can serve the same social purpose as a party.
- Sometimes there is a trade-off between being ef-

ficient and being well liked. When organizing an event or a party, remember your ultimate goal—to meet somebody. Don't concentrate on the logistics or minute details to the extent that your best personal qualities are obscured.

When flying a scheduled airline, try to have your ticket upgraded to first class. And always get dressed nicely—airplanes are a good place to meet eligible men.

Men sometimes approach a woman driving an automobile, asking questions about the car, such as, "What year and model is it? . . . Is your transmission standard or automatic? . . ."

If you find yourself in such a situation, you should know that in most cases, the man has no real interest in the car you're driving. He's interested in *you*. If a man initiates one of these conversations, you should be aware of the following:

- If you're driving a Honda Civic, he's *definitely* interested in you.
- If you're driving a BMW convertible, he's *probably* interested in you.
- If you're driving a Bentley convertible, he's *definitely* interested in you, possibly for the wrong reasons.
- If you're driving a Ferrari Testarossa, he's *definitely* interested in you, and *definitely* interested in the car.

Locating your blanket at the beach is like playing a game of co-ed chess. Before you plunk it down, give some thought to:

- Sitting near men you want to meet
- Avoiding men you don't want to meet
- Anticipating where attractive men will camp out

- If you are athletic, or like athletic men, you might want to locate your blanket near a volleyball or touch-football game. This is not so difficult if a game is already in progress, but if you've never been to a particular beach before, you might ask discreetly in advance where these games will be played. Ask a lifeguard—he or she will know the layout of the beach. Of course, you could locate your blanket anywhere and walk over once the games begin, but then you're being a bit obvious.

• At most beaches equipped with rest rooms, the territory near the facilities tends to be dominated by families with children. The single population generally occupies the territory farther away.

• You can make the forces of nature your ally. The following technique works if you arrive at the beach during low tide.

1. Spot an interesting man whose blanket is located near the waterline.

2. Strategically locate your blanket directly behind his, with enough leeway to allow for the impending rise in tide.

3. When the tide comes in, he will be forced to relocate his blanket in your vicinity. His retreat can be your opportunity.

Some women are uncomfortable socializing in bars in their community, for several reasons. They feel either that the caliber of men they meet will be sub-optimal, or that men will view them in a negative light because "nice women don't go to bars." On vacation, however, bars and nightspots are part of the "experience." There is no stigma attached to being out at a bar, so it's an excellent place to meet quality men.

If you have the inclination and the financial resources, consider taking flying lessons. Not only is it an exhilarating experience, but flying a plane is an activity overwhelmingly populated by men—and upscale men at that. Remember one of the first rules of business—go where the competition isn't.

If a man arranges a date with you but acknowledges that he is simultaneously "seeing someone" it means one of two things. At worst, it means that he is willing to two-time her (and eventually you). At best, it means that you are a "control" in his personal experiment—he is testing the strength of his relationship with her relative to his attraction to you. Proceed at your own risk.

While you may be focused on meeting a man, it's not necessarily a good idea to reveal your focus to the men you meet. Don't launch into questions like "Where do *you* meet people?" or . . . "I've been thinking of joining the Global Gym. What's the male-to-female ratio there?"

Women will often be out and about with groups of friends that include both men and other women. At such times, casual observers, including potential suitors, may not know whether you're paired with one of the men, or whether you're actually available. Therefore, it's your responsibility to make it clear to eligible men that you are, in fact, available. You may have to initiate contact using your eyes, your smile, or by starting a conversation.

Is it OK to try to meet other men when you are on a date? Yes, if

1. You make contact very discreetly.
2. You're certain that you have no interest in ever seeing your current date again.

Chapter 4

Personal Ads

Placing an Ad

Here's a sample ad that's a composite of many that we've seen:

Attractive, divorced, urban professional woman, good sense of humor, loves fine dining, fireplaces, walks on the beach, exotic travel. Comfortable in jeans or evening dress . . . seeks urbane, wealthy, GQ type, 30–35 . . . for serious romance, possibly marriage. Send photo and letter.

Don't be generic. Who doesn't love fine dining, fire-places, and walks on the beach?

Don't be presumptuous. Who'll be paying for the exotic travel?

Don't be offensive. What's your opinion of a man who places an ad for a "statuesque model with cover girl looks"? Men feel the same way about women who advertise for a "wealthy GQ type."

Don't dwell on what you're looking for. Ironically, the additional ad lines that describe your ideal mate not only increase the cost, but actually reduce the number of responses you'll receive.

Be realistic. A wealthy GQ type wouldn't answer an ad that's as generic as the sample above. Which brings us to our next point . . .

Great sense of humor? Don't say it, display it.

If an advertiser with a self-described "great sense of humor" is unable to create an ad containing anything other than a straight compilation of facts and adjectives, a potential respondent will begin to doubt (1) the existence of that great sense of humor and (2) the veracity of the facts and adjectives.

Do emphasize what you have to offer. Use your advertising dollars to publicize your most attractive qualities. This will generate the maximum number of viable responses.

We are always amazed at personal ads that begin "Recently divorced female . . ." Don't label yourself a "divorcée," or use the term anywhere in your ad. Surely there are things about you that are more relevant than this bit of your personal history.

Be certain to mention that you're a female. This may sound obvious, but here is a personal ad that actually appeared recently in a well-known magazine:

Do You Believe in Love?—*If you do, this ad is for you. I am a 27-year-old Jewish educator who still believes* *in love at first sight. I am looking for someone with whom I can spend some quality time, who enjoys Knicks games, candlelit dinners, theater, and walks in the park—or whatever you do (I am spontaneous). If you are 21–33, attractive, athletic, passionate, and affectionate, then we may be ready to share everything life has to offer. Must have sensitive heart and soul, for a meaningful relationship. NYM Box. . . .*

Can you tell whether the advertiser is male or female? We confess that we can't. What we do know is that she/he spent $504 to publicize her/his affinity for professional basketball, candlelight dinners, and the theater. When stating your gender or describing some important personal trait, don't leave your readers guessing.

While you certainly want to present yourself in a favorable light, avoid large stretches of the truth when describing yourself. For the guy on the other end, average may be just fine. When you exaggerate, you set up expectations that will leave him disappointed in your honesty, if nothing else.

After poring over your responses, hopefully you'll hit upon at least two or three that merit a phone call. When you, as an advertiser, call one of your respondents, assume that he may have answered more than one advertisement. As early as possible in the conversation, identify yourself as the "soft-spoken film-maker" or the "green-eyed beauty." You'll get your conversation off to a smoother start, because he won't have to ask awkward questions in an attempt to determine which advertiser you are.

Telephone "voice-mail" personals are becoming increasingly popular. As part of our research for this book, we audited some of these forums, listening to both advertisers and respondents. It was remarkable how few people used the medium to their best advantage. Some advertisers read in a monotone voice from a prepared script, while others stumbled as they spoke.

If you were placing a personal ad in a magazine, you would almost certainly write your message out on paper before calling the ad department, rather than dictating extemporaneously. Since people are so accustomed to using the telephone, it seems that many advertisers in "voice-mail" personals simply pick up the phone and start recording their messages off the top of their head. Don't make this mistake.

In this medium you have a single shot at making your best impression. Be an actress. Use notes if they make you feel more comfortable. Practice your message out loud before you actually record it. You want to sound natural and let your unique personality express itself.

The same rules apply if you're responding to a voice-mail ad.

Responding to an Ad

Beware of long, verbose advertisements. An ad that rambles endlessly about the accomplishments, needs, and wants of the advertiser—in a medium where most advertisers are succinct—usually has an author whose primary (and secondary) interest in life is himself.

Unfortunately, based upon the accounts of our acquaintances, the term "truth in advertising" seems to have evaded a disproportionate number of personal advertisers. Our suggestion: Trust, but verify.

When the advertiser calls, stay on the phone long enough to discern whether the advertised attributes ring true. For example, if the advertiser claims to be a "business tycoon" and his mother answers the phone, don't expect to be picked up in his chauffeur-driven limousine (unless he's the driver).

We've yet to encounter an advertiser (or person, for that matter) who isn't convinced that he has a "great personality," an above-average intellect, and a terrific sense of humor. A few minutes on the phone can authenticate or discredit these claims.

Don't respond to an advertiser with a photocopied form letter or a "mass mailing." If you respond to the personals on a regular basis, you may decide to use a word processor to streamline your task. If you do, modify each of your responses in some way to reflect the uniqueness of each advertiser, and to make it less obvious that you're responding to more than one ad.

If you've answered several ads, set up a system to keep track of the ads you've answered. When the advertiser calls you on the phone, hopefully he'll follow the advice we've outlined above and identify himself, so that you won't be put on the spot. However, if he doesn't identify himself, you have two choices. You can try to guide the conversation in a direction that provides some clues about his identity, or you can admit that you've answered more than one ad (no need to divulge exactly how many) and ask him to identify himself.

Don't respond using company letterhead, unless you own the company.

Some advertisers explicitly request a photo, others leave the request unspoken. If you have a flattering photo to include with your response, *send it*. Almost all male advertisers, even those who don't explicitly request a photo, give first preference to those responses that include one.

Don't take what happens with personal ads personally. The personals are a numbers game. Advertisers—particularly male advertisers—receive dozens of responses. If you don't receive a call-back, it's no reflection on you. Your intent should be simply to make an impression on the advertiser. Don't pour your heart out in a four-page essay in response to any single ad, no matter how appealing the ad sounds. You'll only feel worse if you've invested disproportionate time and energy and receive no response.

Decoding the Language of the Personals

Some terms appear so frequently in the world of the personals (both ads and responses) that we feel obliged to offer some advice regarding the broad spectrum of their interpretations. While some men accurately portray themselves, others take extraordinary "creative license."

Handsome	This represents a broader range of appearance among men than "pretty" does among women.
Unconventionally Handsome	This represents an even broader range of appearance.
Tall	Five foot eight and over.
Successful	Anything from multimillionaire to "employed" (either currently or recently).
Entrepreneur	Could mean anything from captain of industry to owner of a beachfront T-shirt stand.
—look-alike	Tom Selleck, John Travolta, etc. Don't be surprised if the resemblance eludes you.
—need not reply	Fill in some less than desirable attribute, such as "dependent women" or "insecure women." This admonition is often indicative of an arrogant, demanding nature. Perhaps you need *not* reply.
Great legs a plus	Beware of men who are blatantly focused on individual parts of your anatomy.
Great catch	So is a large flounder.

Similarly, when reading your personal ad, men will expect the worst, unless explicitly stated otherwise.

If you don't say "slim" they expect you're not.

If you omit your age, they'll assume you're well beyond the age range they're looking for. Nor is there any point in being vague about your age. If you say "thirties," men will assume you're thirty-eight or thirty-nine.

Most men discount an advertiser's self-description to allow for some exaggeration. When he reads *attractive* he thinks plain; when he reads *pretty* he thinks attractive; when he reads *gorgeous* he thinks pretty. You might want to tailor your ad accordingly.

Chapter 5

Blind Dates

M any women (and men) dread blind dates. They hate the anticipation and the potential for serious disappointment. Our suggestion: Treat blind dates like an airline flight. Normally the passenger sitting next to you is of no consequence, but every now and then . . .

Go on your blind date with no heavy romantic expectations, and perhaps you'll be pleasantly surprised.

Don't confuse a blind date with a real date. You go on a real date with someone you know, like, and expect to enjoy an activity with. In a man's mind, a blind date is more like a "go-see" (a term that describes an initial meeting between a fashion model and a photographer, when the photographer determines whether the model is suitable for the layout he is shooting). Thus, the scheduled activity is less important than the opportunity to meet a prospective companion and determine compatibility.

During the telephone conversation when you discuss the logistics of your meeting, don't suggest cocktails, theater, dinner and dancing. There are several reasons.

1. It's best to start small with drinks or coffee. You want to leave a gracious "way out" for both of you. If things don't work out, you'll each appreciate an opportunity to go your separate ways without recrimination. If things do work out, you'll have plenty of opportunities for more elaborate dates in the future.
2. You don't want to give your date the impression that you can't get a date any other way.

If, on the other hand, a man suggests an overly elaborate evening, you may want to be wary yourself. It's possible that for him, you will be this decade's only link with the female gender.

Don't spend too much time on the phone with a prospective blind date. It's far safer to determine in person whether any chemistry exists between the two of you. Save your time, and avoid setting up unrealistic expectations on both your parts that may get shattered upon meeting.

Some people (both male and female) consider a blind date to be a high-pressure situation that inhibits spontaneous conversation. There's a less pressured way to meet a potential blind date. Request that you both be invited to a social gathering—a friend's party, a dinner at a restaurant, etc. The two of you can be introduced at this event, giving you both an opportunity to chat with each other as much as you'd like. More significantly, if things don't click you can move on and talk to others—an important safety valve and stress reducer.

As the saying goes, "Consider the source."

If a man is setting you up on a blind date, you should be flattered but wary. Sometimes, when men set you up, they are using you as "currency" to show their male friends the caliber of "babe" they can deliver. While you may be flattered to be considered a babe, be aware that your male friend may be more interested in scoring points with his friends than in finding an ideal match for you.

On the other hand, your female friends are more likely to be looking out for your best interests. And if they're close friends, they'll be much more in tune with the type of person you're interested in meeting. Besides, you can be much more blunt in questioning your female friends about your prospective date.

You don't want to be too hasty in eliminating potential sources of blind dates, but consider this: While your contemporaries might share your basic taste in men, people from previous generations (parents, aunts, uncles, etc.) sometimes have a different notion of what an appropriate match for you might be—a notion that might frighten you.

If you are inclined to accept blind dates, consider establishing a historical "file" on your sources. Some sources will consistently come close to the mark, while others will make you wonder what they were thinking or what forgotten grudge against you motivated their recommendation. Making a mental note of your most reliable sources will maximize your chances for success and help avoid disagreeable experiences.

If you haven't been on a date in fourteen months, don't volunteer this information to your prospective blind date.

Chapter 6

Phone Etiquette

It's always better to let the man make the first phone call.

If you subscribe to the theory that women should not make the initial phone call, which we recommend, it's essential to understand the difference between a "call" and a "call-back." Here's an example. If a man gives you his business card and requests that you call him at your convenience, he's *already* called you, by making the initial overture. By phoning him at your convenience, you are, in reality, simply calling him back.

What it means if he doesn't call back:

- If he's genuinely interested, don't worry, he'll call.
- If he's genuinely not interested, it doesn't matter what you do.
- If you sense he *may* be interested (be truthful now), you might as well give him a follow-up call and find out.

When a man calls you for a date, and you say, "I'm busy for the next two weeks, why don't you give me a call after that . . ." don't be surprised if you never hear from him again. For most men, you are essentially saying "No, thank you." Men, even secure men, don't want to set themselves up for a possible second rejection. In this game, it's one strike and you're out.

So if you're interested in the guy, but you really *are* busy for the next two weeks, make sure that you leave no doubt about your interest. You might offer to set a date on the spot, even if the date is two or three weeks away.

There is *no* downside to returning a man's call promptly. It's common courtesy.

If you have call waiting, always give *him* priority. Treat him like a million-dollar customer. If you *must* get back to him (if you really are interrupted by your million-dollar customer), offer to call him back in a short while, then do it.

If you're calling with the intention of setting up a date, make your intention clear. It may help to have a specific activity in mind. Otherwise, you may wind up chatting for ten minutes, he'll wonder why you called, and you'll hang up frustrated.

Answering machines:

- For the first call or two, avoid leaving a message on his answering machine. You can be far more persuasive speaking to him directly.
- Never leave two consecutive unreturned messages on his answering machine.

Chapter 7

Appearance

As people in publishing know (and as we've recently learned), an appealing cover increases the odds that the book will be read.

Honestly assess your strengths and weaknesses. Play to your strengths. Improve, or work around, your weaknesses.

The Dunk Test:

Regardless of how well groomed you are, how much makeup you wear, how well-tailored your Chanel suit, most men are quite skilled at imagining you without your clothes, dunked in a pool of water, free of all accoutrement—in other words, without makeup, hair spray, or contour-enhancing garments. All men do this to a greater or lesser extent, although they might not describe it in precisely these terms.

What does this mean to you? Two things.

1. Get in the best shape you reasonably can.
2. Concentrate on developing and exhibiting those traits that transcend the dunk test . . . your posture, smile, grace, charm, and wit.

There is no downside to being in good shape. Besides, gyms and health clubs are good places to meet men.

Make your posture an asset.

In preparation for this book, we asked our male colleagues about the female attributes that they found most appealing. Surprisingly, the attribute most frequently mentioned was *posture*.

Improving your posture is the most dramatic way to improve your overall appearance. Posture is what men notice *first* about a woman—from a distance of hundreds of feet. Good posture conveys self-confidence as well as sexuality—both appealing characteristics to men.

Jewelry Tips:

- Wear nothing that could possibly be misinterpreted as either a wedding ring or an engagement ring. The type of man you hope to attract will steer clear of any woman who is displaying a tangible commitment to another man. You might go one step further and avoid wearing any rings on the "ring finger" of your left hand.
- Very few women are attractive to men while

wearing as much jewelry as Mr. T. Men are attracted to you, not your jewelry. Jewelry should be complementary, not overwhelming.

You can't change your life by dyeing your hair blond (or any other color). Changing your hair color may be OK as a temporary morale booster, but if men see you with noticeably different color hair every month, it says something about your self-esteem. There is one exception: coloring prematurely gray hair.

Apply whatever makeup it takes to make you look as if you're not wearing any.

Consider getting a *makeover*. When men see these done on television or in their girlfriends' fashion magazines, they are often awestruck by the results.

Fingernails. Emulate the hand close-ups you see in magazines. Not too long, not too short. Definitely not conspicuously bitten. Some men love bright red nail polish, others prefer clear polish or none at all. The color of nail polish is incidental compared with the basic look of the nails.

One possible exception. There may be some men who like big hair, lots of makeup, and superlong fingernails. If that is the type of man you want to attract, fine. But you should realize that in going after this type, you're not casting the widest net possible.

Always wear clean underwear. You never know.

Don't dress to impress other women. Dress to impress men. Only other women know the fashion of the moment. Half the time the current fashion looks outlandish and conceals your physical attributes.

Don't be a fashion victim. Our friends in the fashion industry inform us that it's possible to be stylish, still be appealing to men, and not do major damage to your budget.

If you've got it, flaunt it (but not too flagrantly). If you're comfortable wearing micro-miniskirts or plunging necklines, and can carry it off, fine. If you prefer not to wear high hemlines or low necklines, that's fine, too. But if you've got great legs or curves, don't conceal them under a baggy "fashion statement."

There is no reason to smoke, regardless of what the Virginia Slims ads tell you. Some men don't mind, but most do—even men who smoke themselves.

At the gym:
 We know you're there primarily to work out, and that's commendable. However, don't ignore this opportunity to attract members of the opposite sex.

- Don't wear heavy makeup or jewelry. It looks like you're trying too hard.
- Don't wear baggy sweats.
- Keeping your hair off your face and still looking good is a challenge. Some women look best wearing baseball caps and ponytails; some look best with headbands; still others look best with their hair up in a bun. Experiment with your hair to find the style that looks best on you.

If you are attractive, don't be reluctant to hang out with other attractive women, especially when you've scheduled an evening whose primary agenda is meeting men. In a man's eyes, two women are *more than twice as attractive* as a single woman by herself. You can eliminate the competitive factor by going out with a friend who is already spoken for (boyfriend or husband) and is willing to funnel all the male candidates in your direction.

Put together a "focus group." Manufacturers do this all the time to get the reactions of potential customers to a new product. Solicit the opinions of your male friends. Encourage them to be honest, with no recriminations. You may discover that the hat you think is so chic makes you look like a mushroom (mushrooms reproduce asexually), or that getting a butterfly tattoo on your shoulder may not be such a good idea.

If men find a particular woman sexy or attractive and you can't see it, don't just dismiss their opinion. Ask them why they feel that way. You could acquire some useful insight that you really can't get any other way, certainly not from your girlfriends.

Chapter 8

The First Few Dates

Make sure your body language is consistent with your thoughts.

A polite man will await your nonverbal signal that certain physical barriers have been lifted.

Let a man know you're ready for his physical affection by initiating some form of gentle, subtle, noncommittal physical contact. Taking his hand while walking, or whispering in his ear will signify that it's OK for him to increase the level of physical contact.

Warning! If you are, by nature, a "touchy-feely" person, be advised that such actions can easily be misinterpreted by a man accustomed to acting on non-verbal cues.

Don't stand on ceremony. Even in this day and age, a Saturday-night date is still considered something special. Some people would advise you to refuse, on general principle, any Saturday-night invitation that you receive later than Wednesday. In our view, this restriction is unduly rigid, and adhering to it will eliminate potential opportunities. In contemporary America, most men aren't even aware that such a restriction exists in the minds of some women, and if they were aware, would deliberately eschew women who subscribe to such a rule. On the other hand, a considerate man generally will not call you on Saturday afternoon for a Saturday-evening date.

Don't leave any of your personal items at a man's home. Even if it's unintentional, the man will assume you had an ulterior motive. Even the most piggish of men thinks he knows a little bit of Freudian psychology.

Most men (except those with allergies) would agree that the right perfume can enhance a woman's desirability. One note of caution: Logic might tell you that if a bit of something is good, then a lot is better. This is not the case with perfume.

Many women view their long hair as an asset—and for many women, it is. However, let your hair speak for itself. There is no need to call attention to your hair by stroking it or periodically tossing it over your shoulder—especially on a dinner date.

If you're selecting a restaurant for a dinner date, think twice before suggesting a place where you regularly dine, and are friendly with the maître d', waiters, and staff. A man wants to spend his initial date conversing with you, not catching up on the exploits of your friends at the restaurant.

If a friend or acquaintance materializes while you're on a date, make sure to graciously include your date in any ensuing conversation, or quickly determine your top priority at the moment—your friend or your date. If necessary, graciously excuse yourself and your date. Your friend should understand your desire for privacy.

While we would not presume to tell you what menu items to order on a first date (although healthy dishes will certainly enhance your long-term prospects), there are certain foods you may want to avoid. Poor choices include ribs, barbecued chicken, spaghetti, or any other dish requiring great manual dexterity or a box of Handi-Wipes.

If you'd like him to call you again:

- If you had a good time, say so.
- If you're comfortable with a good-night kiss, go for it.
- If you're more comfortable with a handshake, that's OK, too. You can differentiate your "good-night" handshake from a "business" handshake by clasping a second hand warmly, by prolonging the duration of the handshake, or by accompanying it with extended eye contact or a wink.

Men have a multitude of arbitrary and capricious reasons for rejecting a woman (and vice versa). Little infractions that seem trivial in the context of a long-standing relationship assume monumental proportions during the early dating phase. Be sure to return borrowed items, return his phone calls promptly, and postpone revising his wardrobe or rearranging his kitchen. In the beginning, it's often the little things that can mean the difference between receiving a second call and not.

The first few dates are similar, in some ways, to an employment interview. No candidate volunteers a list of her negative characteristics, so it's up to the interviewer to extrapolate the candidate's potential performance, both positive and negative, from their brief meeting. Men sometimes view your first few dates in much the same way. Since your date knows you won't be admitting your negative characteristics voluntarily, he'll be looking for signals by which he can deduce them. Be aware of the signals you are sending, particularly in the realms of punctuality (did you both miss the play's opening act because you were late?), courtesy (did you neglect to thank him for the theater tickets and dinner?), and responsibility (did you mention that you didn't vote in the last three presidential elections?).

Chapter 9

Date Conversation

Never ask a man to guess your age. There is no upside for you or for him.

- If he guesses too old, he's dead meat, and your self-esteem is diminished.
- If he guesses too young, you know that he probably took his best guess, and was smart enough to subtract a few years.
- If he guesses on the nose, he either didn't subtract enough, or estimated too old in the first place.

While men respect self-confidence, they disdain selfishness. Men are turned off by women who consider themselves the center of the known universe. Try not to start every sentence with the word *I,* or include the words *me* or *my* in every conversation.

The Six-Point World-Awareness Scale:

Whether they articulate it or not, men subconsciously evaluate your level of world awareness relative to their own. Usually they are most comfortable with a level approximating their own level.

Our male colleagues have recounted their conversations with a variety of their dates—women who apparently have run the gamut from "airhead" to corporation president.

For your convenience, we've formalized some of our colleagues' observations in the following Six-Point World-Awareness Scale. Where do you fit in?

- **LEVEL 1** is typified by conversation in which virtually every sentence begins with the pronoun *I:*

  BASIC CONCERNS: Herself and her physical comfort and well-being.

"I love the food at this restaurant. . . . I just went to a Lori Morgan concert, I love her music . . . people say I look like her, what do you think? I think she drives a Jaguar . . . that's my favorite car. An old boyfriend of mine had a silver Jaguar. . . ."

If an amoeba could talk, its conversation would be Level 1.

- **LEVEL 2:**

BASIC CONCERNS: Herself, her family, her friends.

The pronoun *you* is used only to ask what *you* think about *me*.

SAMPLE CONVERSATION

"My father is just the greatest guy. He just bought this new Cadillac and tonight he let me borrow it. Did you see it in the parking lot? It's burgundy with chrome trim. How do you like it?"

- **LEVEL 3:**

BASIC CONCERNS: Herself, her family, her friends, and her date/boyfriend.

She is truly interested in what he thinks about things that are important to her, such as *his* favorite restaurant, sports, and music.

"When I played tennis at my cousin's house last week I tried the new Prince boron graphite racket . . . you should buy one, I think it would be good for your tennis elbow. . . . Have you heard the new Blues Traveler CD? . . . Maybe we should go to their concert next month. . . ."

- ## LEVEL 4:

BASIC CONCERNS: Herself, her family, her friends, and her date/boyfriend.

Also politics, economics, the arts and sciences, but only as they affect herself, her family, and friends.

"The economy is really slowing down . . . my office laid off three people last week, and I've had to pick up their workload. . . . I'm going to a rally next week to protest the waste-treatment plant the city plans to build just two miles from my parents' house."

- ## LEVEL 5:

BASIC CONCERNS: Herself, her family, her friends, and her date/boyfriend.

Also politics, economics, the arts and sciences, as they affect the whole of society.

"The economy is bound to slow down if the Federal Reserve insists on maintaining unrealistically high interest rates . . . if the unemployment rate goes any higher, the homeless shelter where I volunteer is bound to see an increase in its caseload. . . ."

- ## LEVEL 6:

BASIC CONCERNS: Herself, her family, her friends, and her date/boyfriend.

Also politics, economics, the arts and sciences, as they affect the whole of society, with true virtuosity in at least one worldly pursuit.

SAMPLE CONVERSATION

"Good news. My congressional subcommittee has just drafted gun-control legislation that we're sure will be acceptable to both houses of Congress."

Some men at Level 6 might prefer a Level 1 woman, but this is the exception. Most men prefer a world-awareness level that approximates their own.

Decide what you want in a man, and be sure that your conversation reflects it. If you prefer a man at the higher end of the scale, be sure to stay current. Read newspapers and magazines, watch the

Sunday-morning news shows, and familiarize yourself with the events that are shaping the history of
the day.

Men love compliments, especially if they are remotely
plausible. Fortunately, you can take tremendous creative license before a man will sense any exaggeration
on your part.

While various aspects of your life may not be perfect,
don't make your first few dates a forum for your com-
plaints.

During the first few dates is not the time to confess
that you never speak to your parents, have a run-

ning ten-year feud with both your siblings, or that your last three boyfriends were psychopaths. There is no faster way to send a guy packing than to inform him that you have acrimonious relations with the circle of people with whom you should ordinarily be closest.

While modesty and humility are admirable traits, don't be too self-deprecating, even if you do it in a humorous manner. If you knock yourself often enough, the other person may begin to believe you.

There is no downside to being a good person. Don't hesitate to mention the charitable activities that are part of your daily life. If you are a Big Sister or deliver meals to the homebound elderly, that's wonderful—and men will think so, too. It stands to reason that those who would go out of their way for vulnerable strangers would probably be very caring partners.

Men are astounded—and sometimes irked—by women's fascination with our previous relationships. Try to keep your curiosity in check, especially during the first few dates.

Similarly, most men are not especially interested in listening to the history of your relationships, or in hearing about your previous boyfriends.

It's OK to let the man infer that you may be casually dating others. However, if there's a possibility that your relationship with a former love interest might not be over, don't—under any circumstances—volunteer this information to your date. No man wants to invest time and emotional energy establishing a relationship that could be terminated on a moment's notice with a simple "I've gone back to my old boyfriend."

Until you are supremely confident in your relationship, don't tell your prospective boyfriend about your
next-door neighbor who just happens to be a former
cover girl . . . earned her MBA in finance . . . was just
promoted to senior vice president at American Express . . . and is single . . . and looking.

If you've dated a man only once or twice, don't use
the term *relationship* in his presence, to refer to your,
uh, relationship. Some men experience anxiety when
they hear this word too early in a you-know-what.

A man sometimes reacts strangely if he knows too
early that you have a serious interest in him. How,
then, do you encourage him to call you again, without being too obvious? An offer to loan him a book

or an album indicates—at a minimum—that you are open to the idea of seeing him again.

Don't curse or use foul language. Some men might not be put off, but some men will.

Make sure you know your audience before you tell an off-color joke.

Men do not find Lorena Bobbitt jokes amusing.

Men don't find baby talk from female adults endearing.

If you are divorced, don't *define* yourself as a divorcée, either in conversation or in your worldview. Don't dwell on the details of your divorce—this is the last thing in the world most men want to hear about.

Besides, you are a complete person with a career, interests, and abilities that describe you far more comprehensively than the fact that you once had a husband.

If the topic of your divorce is front and center in your conversation, your date may wonder if you are still emotionally connected to your ex, either by virtue of a fond attachment with which your date must compete, or some unresolved anger which he may ultimately experience.

If you have kids . . .

All else being equal, attracting men is sometimes more difficult for women with kids because many men prefer to meet women who are unencumbered by children.

If you have children, mention them relatively early

in the conversation. Obviously they are an important part of your life—more important, hopefully, than your favorite restaurants or movies. If you wait too long or let the man discover your kids for himself (when your son answers the phone), he may resent the manipulation, even if he has no inherent problem dating women with children.

Chapter 10

Dollars and Sense

Some women have been called "dinner professionals" or nicknamed "meals on heels." Don't be one of them.

If a man pays for you on a date, always say, "Thank you."

If you ask *him* out, be prepared to pay for the date. (You probably won't have to.)

If you sense that a man sees you as *his* meal ticket, consider moving on.

When a man steadfastly insists on paying for *everything,* despite your offers to share expenses, beware. He usually expects something in exchange.

If the man *always* pays for *everything* (because you don't offer to share expenses), there's a strong possibility that you don't have a relationship, but rather a string of dates.

Don't leave the restaurant while your date is still doing the paperwork on the American Express bill.

If the man is paying, don't order an eighteen-dollar glass of wine and take just one sip. Think twice about ordering an excessively expensive glass of wine in the first place—it sends a message.

There is *no* downside to offering to pay your share.

If you're not going to split expenses down the middle, try one of these three options:

- Offer to pay at least a token expense, such as cab fare or coffee. Do this by the second date. If you wait for the fourth date to do this, there might not be one.
- When the check arrives, words to the effect of "Can I contribute something?" will be greatly appreciated.
- Discuss it. Say something like "This is all so confusing in this day and age, I never know what to do; . . . if you'd like, I'll pay my share, pay the tip, I'll even pay for you. . . ." Said gracefully, this is both charming and memorable.

Don't let him know you're interested in his money, even if you are. Men who actually *have* enough money to warrant that interest live in fear of that possibility.

However, for those of you who *are* interested in a man with money, here's a tip. Men with money usu-

ally wear custom suits. One way to identify a custom
suit is by its cuffs—the cuffs have real buttonholes and
the buttons actually work (as opposed to an off-the-
rack suit, where the cuff buttons are merely decora-
tive).

If you are on an encounter that is not "officially" a
date, but you're with a man you might like to date in
the future—say you're sharing a taxi home after a
party—always offer to pay your share. If the man has
any interest, he'll appreciate the gesture of indepen-
dence and courtesy. Incidentally, he'll almost always
decline your offer to pay.

Men don't necessarily seek financial equality in
women, just evidence that they are self-sufficient and
reliable.

Attempt to keep your finances in reasonable order. Men see your fiscal irresponsibility as a liability that will ultimately be a drain on them.

Never admit that you are financially dependent on your parents. No man wants to assume the role of daddy.

Is a woman's financial situation important to a man?

In its 1996 Valentine's Day edition, the *Wall Street Journal* reported that dual-income households have become the rule rather than the exception in America today. Therefore, men increasingly are required to view a woman's financial situation in the same way that women have traditionally viewed a man's.

How have women traditionally viewed a man's financial situation? Look at the personal ads in any major magazine or newspaper. These are a genuine barometer of women's attitudes. When women advertisers are actually paying for their requests, truth becomes more important than diplomacy. In any week's personal ads, note the number of female advertisers who directly request "successful . . . financially secure . . . established" men. As the saying goes, this is where the rubber meets the road.

You can arrange your finances any way you choose: frugally, frivolously, or somewhere in between—the choice is yours. However, be aware that there are certain indicators that give men pause.

- Is the woman unnecessarily living paycheck to paycheck?
- Is she overdrawn on her credit cards?
- Are her savings less important than her next vacation?
- Are her stated lifestyle expectations out of sync with her financial situation?

If the answers are yes to these questions, it will be clear to any seriously interested man that, ultimately, he will be responsible for keeping the two of you solvent.

So if you are financially challenged, don't volunteer it. It's better to be viewed as an asset than a liability. In today's world, most men are seeking a partner, not a passenger.

A few words about gifts . . .

If you receive nothing on Valentine's Day, it's *not* a good sign.

When you give a gift, *meaningful* is more important than expensive.

Consider giving him a bottle of cologne that you know will make you want to attack him. (Just kidding!)

Don't try to change him with your gifts. For example, gold cuff links for a man whose basic wardrobe consists of jeans and sweatsuits might be too much of a stretch.

Transportation Etiquette: Automobiles and Elevators

If you do nothing else, remember this. If the man opens and closes the car door for you, *make certain* to reach over and unlock the door on his side of the car, before he gets there. Believe it or not, failure to perform this simple act can disqualify a woman from further consideration in the eyes of many men.

Never criticize his driving. Advising him to wear a seat belt is the only exception.

Know how to read a road map. Juggling a large folded piece of paper and the steering wheel at the same time is difficult. When the man is driving, he'll appreciate any assistance you can render in this regard. This capability (in our experience, one acquired by few women) adds an aura of competence, one far in excess of the assistance you've actually rendered.

When the man is driving you, offer to pay the tolls. It's not so much the money that he'll care about, but he'll appreciate your sparing him the inconvenience of reaching into his pocket to retrieve his wallet while driving. He probably won't accept, but your gesture will be appreciated and remembered.

Try not to fall asleep in the car. Many men will interpret your nap as a reflection of a lack of interest.

In addition, it's not the most flattering state in which to be viewed.

When exiting a crowded elevator, courteous men often let all the women exit first. If your escort is among the last men to exit, be sure that you wait near the elevator door to rejoin him. Don't keep walking and let him race to catch up with you twenty yards down the hallway.

Chapter 12

Rejection: Giving and Receiving

It's said that everybody knows somebody who knows somebody who knows the President. Rest assured that in your community, any desirable man knows somebody who knows somebody who knows the guy you're about to reject.

Therefore, when declining an invitation, or ending a series of dates, be compassionate—certainly for humanitarian reasons, and also to serve your own best interests.

In declining an invitation for a date, compassion is sometimes a greater virtue than truth.

Saying "I have a boyfriend" is a firm yet diplomatic way to halt the advances of all but the most persistent pursuer. Even if it's a white lie, it puts a quick end to the advance without any acrimony.

On the other hand, the very same line can be insulting if you've just spent the last ninety minutes flirting with a guy, who was logically assuming you were available.

Saying "I'm so wrapped up in my work right now that I can't consider dating" sends the message that your reluctance to date a particular gentleman is no reflection on him.

On the other hand, if your life is genuinely complicated but you don't want to discourage his pursuit, don't go on and on about how overworked you are at the office.

What's one of the best ways to terminate a nascent relationship after just one or two dates with a nice guy who's just not your type? Tell the man, "I know a friend who's perfect for you" (assuming you actually know such a person). In this way you're enlarging your circle of friends, while presumably doing your girlfriend a favor. Finally, the man may know a friend for you.

What's another way? The (surprisingly) fragile male ego can accept the fact that you've gotten back together with an old boyfriend. Make use of this if you find it too difficult to tell him straight out that he's not for you.

Sometimes, when you're on the phone arranging the logistics of a date with a man you haven't yet met in person, it becomes obvious simply from the conversation that it's not going to work. In this case you can be very forthright. You can honestly say, "This doesn't appear to be clicking," without offending the man. You'll save time and avoid irritation for both of you.

When you're certain that you have no interest in a particular man, avoid the following, which are neither truthful nor compassionate.

- When he asks for your phone number, don't give him your phone number with an intentionally incorrect digit.
- When he calls, don't say, "I'll get back to you tomorrow," if you have no intention of calling, hoping he will get the message.
- When he calls, don't say, "I'm on call waiting, I'll call you right back," and never call back.

Never reject a potential date because you think he doesn't meet the standards established by your friends. It's difficult enough for a man to live up to *your* expectations, let alone the collective expectations of your circle of friends.

It's not always better to give than to receive.

Let's say you've just completed your first or second date. You felt no chemistry between you and you're convinced that your date felt the same way. Minimize your anxiety and discomfort by allowing him to "reject" you first.

If, after just a few dates, you or the man chooses to terminate the relationship, neither owes the other a detailed explanation or postmortem. At this juncture, enumeration of the other's fatal flaws is generally not appreciated as constructive advice.

Words you'll hear if a man is not interested:

- "Let me check my schedule and get back to you in a few days."
- "I hope you enjoy that trip abroad you'll be taking next summer" (if these are his parting words after your first date, and it's November).
- "I had a good time. Maybe I'll see you . . . at the mall . . . around the campus . . . at the gym. . . . (Fill in whatever you want. The word *maybe* indicates that you shouldn't bank on seeing him again anytime soon).

Rejection comes with the dating territory. Here are a few maxims to make the point:

- In baseball, even the best hitter fails 70 percent of the time.

- No pain, no gain.
- No risk, no reward.
- You've got to be in it to win it.

You get the idea. It's better to risk the possibility of discomfort than to stay home every weekend.

Chapter 13

Miscellaneous Advice

Don't be a man's first date after he's just ended a long-term relationship. Unless you were the cause of the relationship's demise, you're just the "control" in his dating experiments. Let somebody else have that honor.

There is *no* downside to being punctual.

Don't date a co-worker unless you plan to marry him, or you both work for an enormous company.

How do you treat waiters, cabbies, doormen? Any arrogance you exhibit toward others will eventually be directed toward the man in your life. Men know this.

Don't date married men. Period.

Don't date if *you* are married. If you're married, close this book and give it to one of your single friends.

A Final Thought

As a wise man (or woman) once said: "It isn't the mountains ahead that will wear you out—it's the grain of sand in your shoe." It's been our intention throughout this book to help you eliminate those nagging grains of sand that impede your success in attracting, dating, and initiating relationships with men. Remember, small changes can make a difference that will last a lifetime.

Now that you know all of our secrets, use them to your best advantage. The male team is on the field, and you've got their playbook. Good luck!

The Best LOVE *The Best* SEX

Creating
Sensuous, Soulful,
Supersatisfying
Relationships

Suzi Landolphi

PUTNAM